The Big Rebou

Knights VS Dragons

Hello sports fans! The game is tied at 2 goals each with only minutes left in this championship soccer game. The fans are on the edge of their seats. Will the Knights or the Dragons score the next goal to win the game? Wow, we are in for an exciting finish as both teams are playing well. The players are ready as the game is set to resume, so let's check out the action between the Knights and the Dragons.

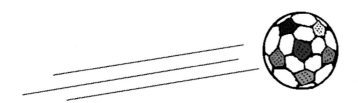

ISBN 978-0-9808866-1-0

Practice early reading skills using the special page format.
- see our Literacy Guide on page 54 -

Support the literacy development of all children.
www.boysRreading.com

ColorSports Publishing Inc.

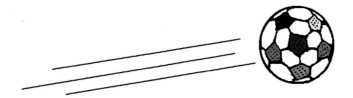

ColorSports Publishing Inc. - 5 Livingstone Dr. - Dundas - L9H 7S3 - Ontario - Canada

Printed in China

Welcome soccer fans, kids, parents, grammas and gramps.
Who will win this big game and be this year's new champs?

Will the Knights win the game, wearing their white, blue and gold?
They play the game so skillfully and always brave and bold.

But the red, white and black play with a strong desire to win.
These Dragons seem to fly and breathe out fire from within.

The game is tied at two goals each, with five minutes left to go.
Let's catch up with the action, as the excitement begins to grow.

1

A a
B b
C c
D d
E e
F f
G g
H h
I i
J j
K k
L l
M m
N n
O o
P p
Q q
R r
S s
T t
U u
V v
W w
X x
Y y
Z z

TOYS TOYS · REDUCE·REUSE·RECYCLE · THE FINAL MINUTES 03:00 → 02:00 → 01:00 → 00:00 · World Peace · FAST ACT

The Dragons race downfield,
as the fans make some noise.

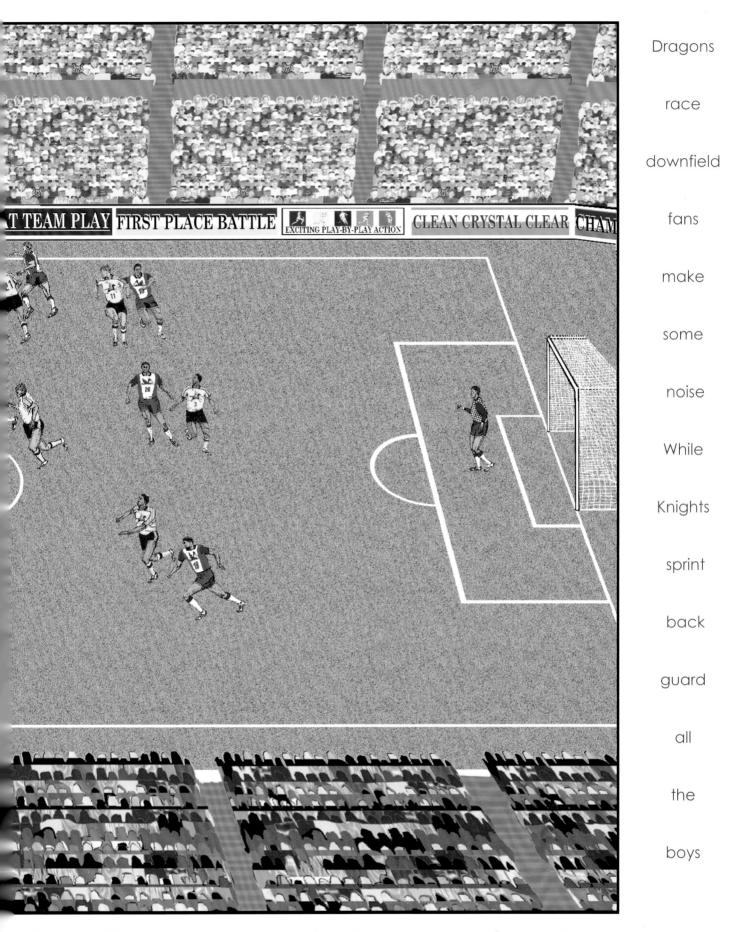

While the Knights sprint back
to guard all the boys.

A a
B b
C c
D d
E e
F f
G g
H h
I i
J j
K k
L l
M m
N n
O o
P p
Q q
R r
S s
T t
U u
V v
W w
X x
Y y
Z z

A Dragon waits with the ball
ready to make the throw.

Dragon waits with ball ready make throw His teammate breaks free excitement starts grow

His teammate breaks free as the excitement starts to grow.

5

A a
B b
C c
D d
E e
F f
G g
H h
I i
J j
K k
L l
M m
N n
O o
P p
Q q
R r
S s
T t
U u
V v
W w
X x
Y y
Z z

Every Knight finds a Dragon,
to follow and to guard.

For the Dragons have the ball,
charging fast and hard.

The Dragon crosses the ball with a well placed kick.

Dragon crosses ball with well placed kick Then his striker volleys with precise head flick

Then his striker volleys it with a precise head flick.

9

A a
B b
C c
D d
E e
F f
G g
H h
I i
J j
K k
L l
M m
N n
O o
P p
Q q
R r
S s
T t
U u
V v
W w
X x
Y y
Z z

© C. HICKS / 2002

The goalkeeper lunges as
the fans watch in disbelief.

goalkeeper lunges fans watch in disbelief slaps ball away Oooh They sigh in big relief

He slaps the ball away!
Oooh! They sigh in big relief!

A a
B b
C c
D d
E e
F f
G g
H h
I i
J j
K k
L l
M m
N n
O o
P p
Q q
R r
S s
T t
U u
V v
W w
X x
Y y
Z z

A Knight back kicks the ball
away, no more scoring chance

Knight

back

kicks

ball

away

no

more

scoring

chances

midfield

players

race

upfield

play

advances

The midfield players race upfield, as the play advances.

A a
B b
C c
D d
E e
F f
G g
H h
I i
J j
K k
L l
M m
N n
O o
P p
Q q
R r
S s
T t
U u
V v
W w
X x
Y y
Z z

© C. HICKS / 2002

The Dragon players begin
to retreat, all moving back.

Dragon players begin retreat all moving back As Knight forwards control ball mounting an attack

As the Knight forwards control the ball, mounting an attack.

A   a
B   b
C   c
D   d
E   e
F   f
G   g
H   h
I   i
J   j
K   k
L   l
M   m
N   n
O   o
P   p
Q   q
R   r
S   s
T   t
U   u
V   v
W   w
X   x
Y   y
Z   z

The Knight striker kicks a quick shot, trying to win the match.

16

Knight striker kicks quick shot trying to win match Dragon keeper ready makes easy catch

But the Dragon keeper is ready and makes an easy catch.

17

© C. HICKS/2002

Hoof! A good solid kick by the Dragon goalkeeper.

Hoof good solid kick by Dragon goalkeeper aims way downfield trying get the ball deeper

He aims way downfield, trying to get the ball deeper.

A a
B b
C c
D d
E e
F f
G g
H h
I i
J j
K k
L l
M m
N n
O o
P p
Q q
R r
S s
T t
U u
V v
W w
X x
Y y
Z z

The players track the ball,
then three of them jump.

players track ball then three of them jump Dragon heads ball passing it with thump

A Dragon heads the ball,
passing it with a thump.

A a
B b
C c
D d
E e
F f
G g
H h
I i
J j
K k
L l
M m
N n
O o
P p
Q q
R r
S s
T t
U u
V v
W w
X x
Y y
Z z

A Dragon forward takes the pass, moving to his right.

Dragon forward takes pass moving to his right faces two Knight fullbacks their net sight

He faces two Knight fullbacks, but has their net in sight.

A a
B b
C c
D d
E e
F f
G g
H h
I i
J j
K k
L l
M m
N n
O o
P p
Q q
R r
S s
T t
U u
V v
W w
X x
Y y
Z z

With a challenge from each side, he looks for an open spot

With

challenge

from

each

side

looks

open

spot

Knight

goalkeeper

ready

Will

Dragon

take

shot

The Knight goalkeeper is ready.
Will this Dragon take a shot?

A a
B b
C c
D d
E e
F f
G g
H h
I i
J j
K k
L l
M m
N n
O o
P p
Q q
R r
S s
T t
U u
V v
W w
X x
Y y
Z z

Yes! The ball rockets toward the net, a kick indeed well struck.

Yes

ball

rockets

toward

net

kick

well

struck

Wow

Knight

keeper

save

little

bit

luck

Wow! The Knight keeper makes he save, with a little bit of luck.

The Dragon takes the corner kick, sending it right in.

Dragon takes corner kick sending right in ball flies high rising quick bending with spin

The ball flies high, rising quick, bending with a spin.

A a
B b
C c
D d
E e
F f
G g
H h
I i
J j
K k
L l
M m
N n
O o
P p
Q q
R r
S s
T t
U u
V v
W w
X x
Y y
Z z

The Dragon forwards move right in, ready to get the ball.

Dragon forwards move right ready get ball Knight keeper leaps high steals from them all

But the Knight keeper leaps so high, he steals it from them all.

A a
B b
C c
D d
E e
F f
G g
H h
I i
J j
K k
L l
M m
N n
O o
P p
Q q
R r
S s
T t
U u
V v
W w
X x
Y y
Z z

The crowd cheers for the keepe
his saves were astounding.

crowd

cheers

for

keeper

his

saves

were

astounding

now

kicks

ball

away

giving

good

pounding

He now kicks the ball away,
giving it a good pounding.

A Knight forward meets the ball, as it falls from the sky.

Knight forward meets ball it falls from sky controls great skill taking with his thigh

He controls it with great skill, taking it with his thigh.

A a
B b
C c
D d
E e
F f
G g
H h
I i
J j
K k
L l
M m
N n
O o
P p
Q q
R r
S s
T t
U u
V v
W w
X x
Y y
Z z

He spots a Knight upfield, and leads him nicely with a pass.

spots

Knight

upfield

leads

him

nicely

pass

Kicking

ball

up

ahead

quickly

rolls

along

grass

Kicking the ball up ahead, it quickly rolls along the grass.

A a
B b
C c
D d
E e
F f
G g
H h
I i
J j
K k
L l
M m
N n
O o
P p
Q q
R r
S s
T t
U u
V v
W w
X x
Y y
Z z

Sprinting toward the Dragon net, two Knights break right in.

Sprinting toward Dragon net Knights break in Trying hard score next goal give team win

Trying hard to score the next goal, to give their team the win.

A a
B b
C c
D d
E e
F f
G g
H h
I i
J j
K k
L l
M m
N n
O o
P p
Q q
R r
S s
T t
U u
V v
W w
X x
Y y
Z z

Boom! A Knight kicks a hard shot and the goalkeeper dives

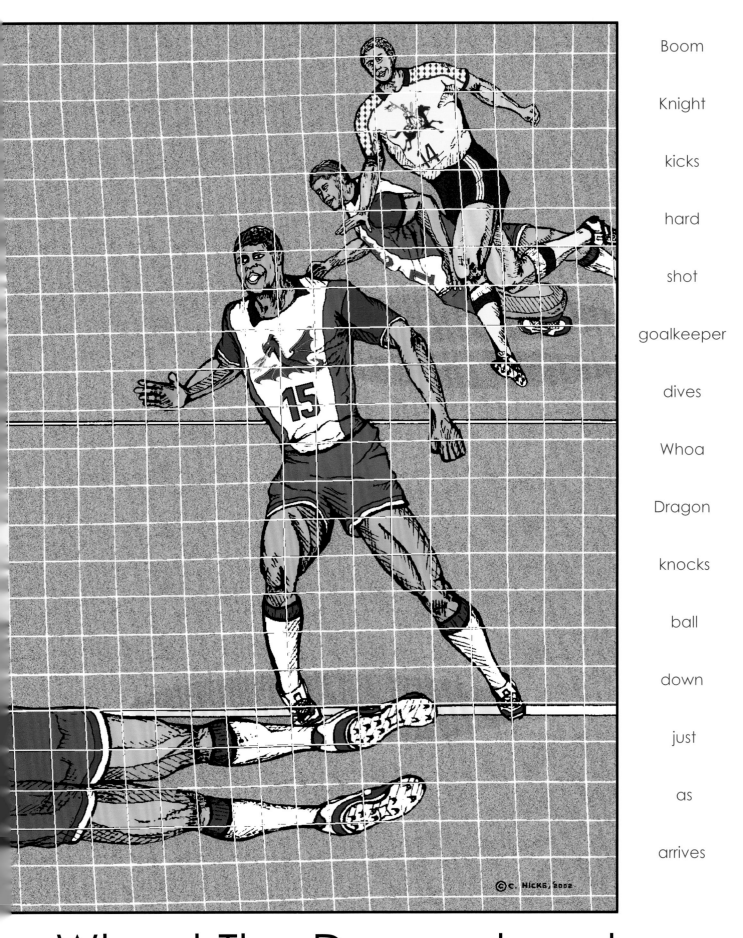

Boom

Knight

kicks

hard

shot

goalkeeper

dives

Whoa

Dragon

knocks

ball

down

just

as

arrives

Whoa! The Dragon knocks
the ball down just as it arrives.

A a
B b
C c
D d
E e
F f
G g
H h
I i
J j
K k
L l
M m
N n
O o
P p
Q q
R r
S s
T t
U u
V v
W w
X x
Y y
Z z

Wow! What a save, the loose ball now rolls along the ground

Wow

What

save

loose

ball

now

rolls

along

ground

players

scramble

fast

get

big

rebound

The players scramble so fast
to get the big rebound.

43

A a
B b
C c
D d
E e
F f
G g
H h
I i
J j
K k
L l
M m
N n
O o
P p
Q q
R r
S s
T t
U u
V v
W w
X x
Y y
Z z

Whoosh! A Knight kicks the ball past the keeper. HE SCORES!

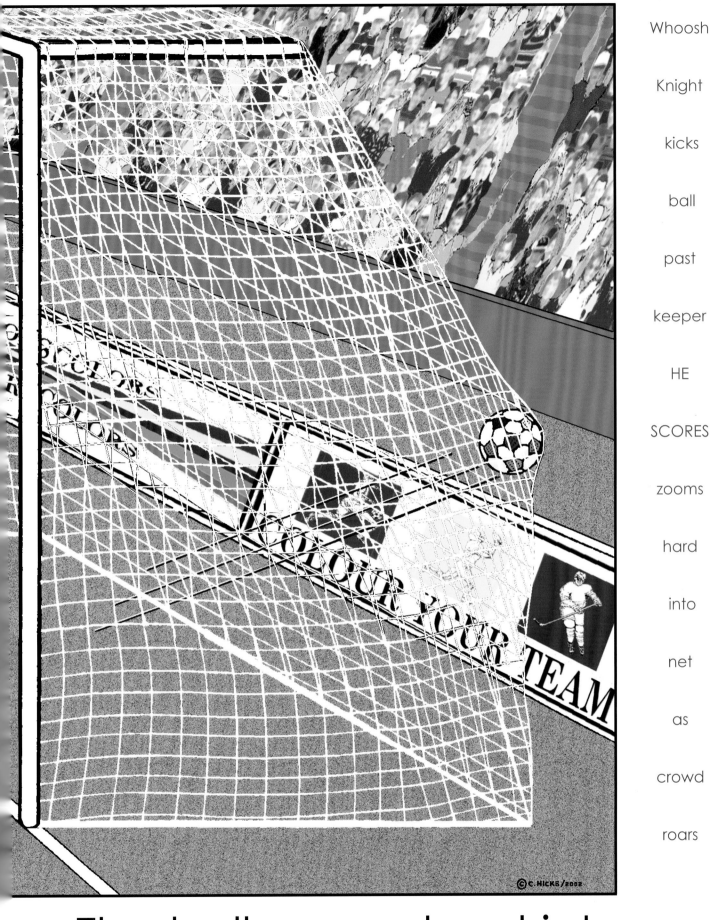

Whoosh Knight kicks ball past keeper HE SCORES zooms hard into net as crowd roars

The ball zooms hard into the net, as the crowd roars.

A a
B b
C c
D d
E e
F f
G g
H h
I i
J j
K k
L l
M m
N n
O o
P p
Q q
R r
S s
T t
U u
V v
W w
X x
Y y
Z z

Wow! The Knights have scored and now the time runs out.

Wow Knights have scored now time runs out Knights win game their fans scream shout

The Knights win the game and their fans scream and shout.

The Dragons and Knights were locked in competition.
Moving upfield and downfield, a grand exhibition.

The players fought hard with no energy to spare.
In the heat of the battle they always played fair.

The players now walk about and greet one another.
They reach to shake hands showing respect for each other.

Yes, winning the championship is a sensation.
And playing with sportsmanship wins admiration.

Soccer Player Positions

wards: - center forward, right forward, left forward, right winger, left winger

The players who make up the attacking line or forward line of a team, the center forward, right forward, left forward, right winger and the left winger. These forwards will work together controlling and passing the ball to each other. They will try to get into a position to shoot the ball on the net to try and score a goal. These players are often the fastest players and best dribblers on a team.

dfielders: - center halfback, right halfback, left halfback

The three halfback players who play behind the forwards but in front of the fullbacks, the defenders. They support the forwards when their team is attacking and trying to score and will support the fullbacks and goalkeeper when their team is defending, trying to prevent the other team from scoring.

fenders: - right fullback, left fullback, goalkeeper

The players who play back during the action of a soccer game to defend their zone and goal. They try to stop a goal from being scored and prevent any scoring chances. They check and cover the opposition players who are attacking and trying to score a goal.

alkeeper:

The player who plays in the goal. He is positioned directly in front of the goal and tries to prevent the ball from getting into the net behind him. This is the only player allowed to use his hands and arms to play the ball to prevent the other team from scoring a goal.

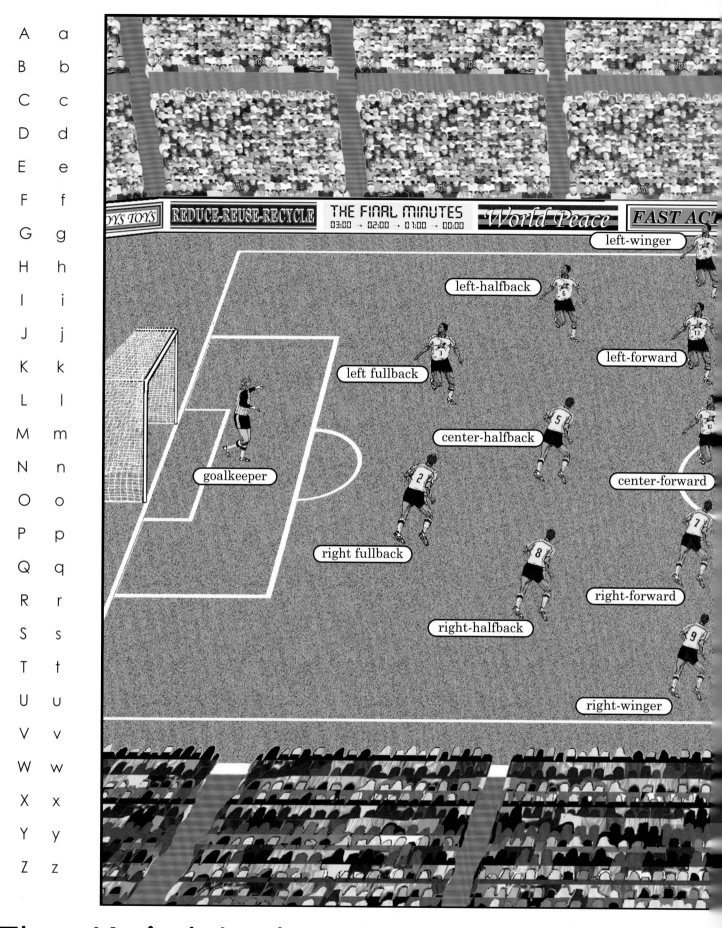

The Knight players move forwar
to set up their plan.

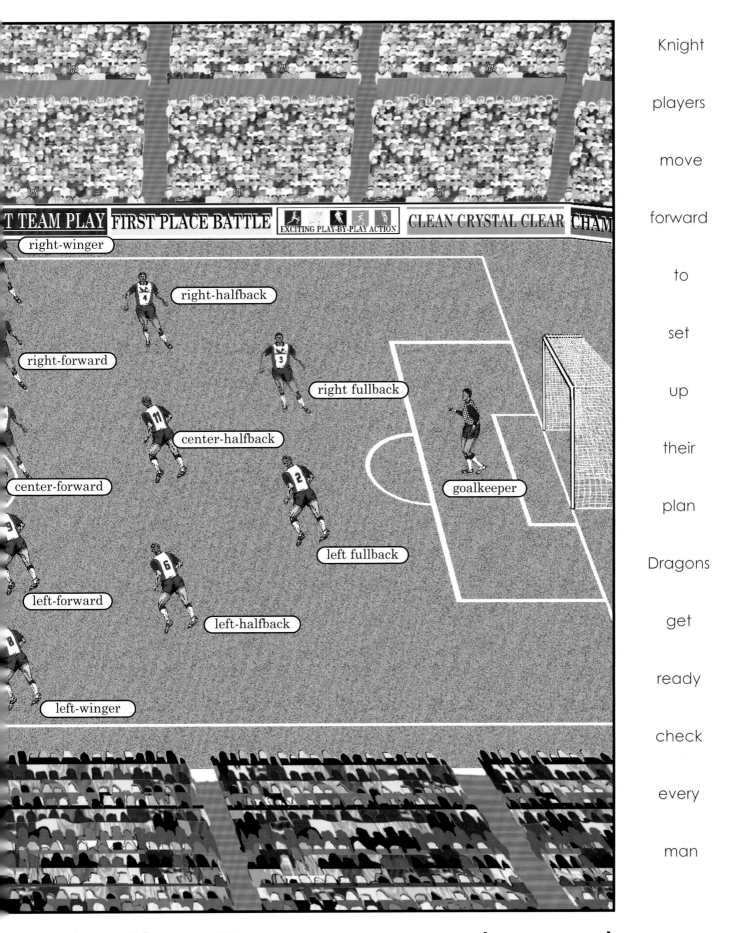

As the Dragons get ready
to check every man.

Soccer Glossary

Attack: To advance the ball into your opponents zone in an effort to score a goal.

Attacking team: The team that has possession of the ball.

Bending with a spin: When the soccer ball flies through the air in a curved direction, the spinning of the ball causes it to move to the left or the right.

Break clear: When a player gets to open space to receive a pass or dribble the ball enabling their team to quickly advance the ball down the field.

Challenge: When a player attempts to stop or take the ball away from a player with possession the ball.

Control the ball: When a player has control of the ball with his feet, dribbling the ball.

Corner kick: When the ball is kicked from the corner in an attempt to score a goal. The attacking team gets a corner kick when the ball crosses the goal line after being touched by the defending team.

Cross or crossing pass: A pass from an attacking player to a teammate in the middle of the field near the goal area, used to give the teammate a good scoring opportunity.

Defenders: The players on the team that try to prevent a goal from being scored on their team. They do not have possession of the ball.

Dribbling: The skill of controlling the ball with the feet while advancing the ball.

Drop kick: When a goalie drops the ball from his hands and kicks it as it falls to his feet.

Field: The rectangular area where a soccer game is played.

Foul: When a player breaks one of the rules for which the referee awards a free kick to the other team.

Goal: A goal is scored when the ball goes between the posts into the net.

Goalkeeper: (goalie) The player who guards the net to prevent the opponents from scoring a goal by stopping the ball any way he can.

Hand ball: A foul when a player touches the ball with his hand or arm. The opposing team is awarded a free kick.

Header: When a player uses his head to contact the ball to control it.

Lead pass: A ball kicked ahead to a teammate running ahead to lead him and advance the ball.

Net: The netting attached to the frame of the goal to trap the ball when a goal is scored.

ide: An attacking player cannot advance forward without the ball unless an opposing defensive player is between him and the goal he is attacking.

en spot: A part of the net that is open, not blocked by the goalkeeper, giving an attacking player a chance to score a goal.

alty: A punishment given by the referee for a violation of the rules.

alty shot: A kick taken by a player against the opposing goalie without any players closer than 10 yards away.

advances: When the ball is kicked forward into the opponents end to set up a scoring chance.

sing: When a player kicks the ball to his teammate to move the ball closer to the opposing goal to score a goal or keep the ball away from an opponent.

ree: The official in a soccer game. The referee watches all the action closely to make sure all the rules are followed so the game is played fairly. They watch for and call any fouls and make decisions about goals scored.

eat: When all the players of a team run back towards their own zone to defend their goal.

e: When a goalkeeper blocks or stops the soccer ball from going into his team's net.

res: When a player kicks the ball into the net of the opposing team for a goal.

t: A ball kicked or headed by a player at the opponent's net trying to score a goal.

line: The boundary line that runs the length of the field along each side. A ball is out of play when it crosses the sideline and is out of bounds.

l: When a player takes the ball away from an opposing player.

er: A team's strongest forward who plays in the center of the field and tries to score goals.

eper: A defender that plays close to his own goal behind the rest of the defenders and in front of the goalkeeper.

kling: When a player takes the ball away from another player by kicking or stopping it with his feet.

w-in: When a player throws the ball from behind his head with two hands while standing behind a sideline. A throw-in is taken by a player opposite the team that last touched the ball before it went out of bounds.

ey: When the ball is in the air and is played by a player with his foot or head.

struck: When a player kicks the ball with great force making good contact with his foot.

Literacy Guide

Practice early reading skills using the special page format.

The special page format is designed to enhance the opportunity for children to practice key skills in their reading development. The chart below highlights 4 specific skills that are fundamental building blocks required to produce a new reader. Along with the story text in black at the bottom of each story scene there are letters in blue on the left and words in red on the right as a quick and handy reference to practice some of these skills.

Use their current ability as a guide to focus on the appropriate skills to practice.

4 Building Blocks Of Reading - With Suggested Reading Skills Activities

Oral Language Development

Speaking aloud and expressing ideas and thoughts builds oral language skills and provides an essential foundation for the development of reading.

Suggested Activities

- look through the story letting the child talk and tell about the pictures using their own words

- encourage, listen and actively respond to the child's own words, thoughts and ideas

- prompt for more oral discussion and detail with questions and rephrasing their words and ideas

- take turns talking about the action and what the players and fans might be feeling, thinking and saying

Letter and Sound Recognition

An essential pre-reading skill is recognizing all the letters (upper and lower case) of the alphabet and the sounds that they make.

Suggested Activities

- together point to each blue letter, name and make the sound of each letter in the alphabet

- explain letters have a lower case (small) symbol and upper case (big) symbol

- name a letter, the sound it makes and then have your child point to it (take turns making it a fun game)

- identify a letter and see if it can be found in a red word on the left and in the story (letters make words)

Building Word Vocabulary

An important reading skill development is the ability to visually identify words, to recognize the grouping of letters and to remember the word meaning.

Suggested Activities

- point to and say a red word, name each letter and their sounds that group together making each word

- point to and read a red word and then let your child find it in the story sentence (take turns making it a game)

- take turns pointing to and reading aloud each red word from the top to bottom in order

- point to a red word, have your child say the word and explain its meaning (make a sentence with the word)

Reading Fluency and Comprehension

Developing the ability to read words accurately and understand their meaning at the same time produces a fluent and competent reader.

Suggested Activities

- read the story together, develop a rhythm and use the rhyme to create and model a natural reading fluency

- ask questions about the action and events to check for memory and understanding

- discuss the thinking, emotions and feelings of the many players and spectators watching the game

- talk about team work, fair-play and sportsmanship, allowing your child to express their feelings and ideas

Find a good balance between working with your child's current abilities and challenging them to learn

Please support the literacy development of your child.